S0-BDM-831

PEEPS®, the PEEPS® Chick Shape, the PEEPS® Bunny Shape, and PEEP ON A PERCH™ are trademarks of Just Born, Inc., Bethlehem, PA, USA and are used under license. © 2018. All rights reserved. Published in the United States by Random House Children's Books, a division of Penguin Random House LLC, 1745 Broadway, New York, NY 10019, and in Canada by Penguin Random House Canada Limited, Toronto. Random House and the colophon are registered trademarks of Penguin Random House LLC.

rhcbooks.com

ISBN 978-1-5247-7054-9

Designed by Diane Choi

MANUFACTURED IN CHINA

10 9 8 7 6 5 4 3 2 1

A SWEET EASTER TRADITION

PEEP ON A PERCH ™

By Andrea Posner-Sanchez Illustrated by Jannie Ho

RANDOM HOUSE 🏠 NEW YORK

Everyone knows the Easter Bunny leaves surprises for girls and boys to discover on Easter. But did you know the Easter Bunny has very special helpers?

They are the Easter Peeps!
And your Easter Peep has come to spend springtime with you.

Easter Peeps have many important jobs. With paints and dyes of all colors, they help turn plain eggs into . . .

. . . spectacular eggs!

Easter Peeps also take
empty Easter baskets . . .

. . . and fill them with all kinds of treats!

But your Easter Peep's most important job is keeping an eye on you!

In the days and weeks leading up to Easter, your Easter Peep watches to make sure you are being good and kind.

Your Easter Peep notices every time you speak and act politely, treat others with kindness, and help around the house.

The nicer you are, the happier your
Easter Peep is!

And when your Easter Peep tells the Easter Bunny how good you are, they might choose to add extra treats to your basket or hide a super-special egg for you to find.

So place your Easter Peep on a perch in your home—any flat surface, such as a windowsill, bookshelf, or table, will do.

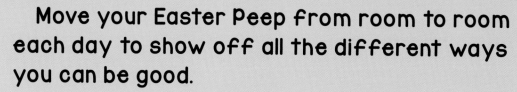

Move your Easter Peep from room to room each day to show off all the different ways you can be good.

Sit properly for meals in the dining room.

Feed the dog in the kitchen.

Read to your baby brother in the living room.

And then, on Easter morning, the fun comes!
How many hidden eggs can you find? What
goodies are in your basket?

Thank your Easter Peep—and the Easter Bunny—for all your treats. They'll be back again next year to celebrate how good you are.

Remember to always be sweet, like a Peep!

And have a very
Happy Easter!